The *Hungry* Black Bag

ANN TOMPERT *Illustrated by* JACQUELINE CHWAST

HOUGHTON MIFFLIN COMPANY BOSTON 1999

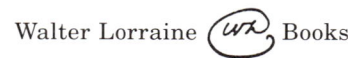

Walter Lorraine (wr) Books

Text Copyright © 1999 by Ann Tompert
Illustrations Copyright © 1999 by Jacqueline Chwast

All rights reserved. For information about permission to reproduce selections from this book, write to Permissions, Houghton Mifflin Company, 215 Park Avenue South, New York, New York.

Library of Congress Cataloging-in-Publication Data
Tompert, Ann.
  The hungry black bag / written by Ann Tompert : illustrated by Jacqueline Chwast.
      p.   cm.
  Summary: Meeting several animals on their way to market, greedy Ole Goat takes their wares for his hungry black bag, but he suffers an unfortunate fate when he tries to take Bear's hat.
   ISBN 0-395-89418-2
   (1. Greed—Fiction.   2. Goats—Fiction.   3. Animals—Fiction.
I. Chwast, Jacqueline, ill.   II. Title.
PZ7.T598Mu   1999
[E]—DC21   98-36195
                                                            CIP
                                                             AC

Printed in the United States of America
WOZ 10 9 8 7 6 5 4 3 2 1

It was market day. Everyone from miles around was carting things to the town square to sell. Ole Goat of Grede Mountain left his rocky lair and trotted down the long, narrow trail that wound around the mountain to the valley below. He dragged his black bag behind him and bellowed,

"I have mountains of stuff.
But that's not enough.
I want more, more, more!"

He had not gone far when he came upon Owl balancing a table on his head.

"My bag is hungry," said Ole Goat. "Give me your table or I'll pitch you down the mountain with my bony, bony head."

"They say you have dozens of tables already," protested Owl. "You don't need mine."

Ole Goat pawed the ground and lowered his head.

"But I want more," bellowed Ole Goat as he charged toward Owl.

Owl threw the table to the ground and skedaddled down the trail. Ole Goat put the table into his black bag.

Ole Goat of Grede Mountain trotted down the trail until he came to Fox pulling a cart heaped with rag rugs and quilts.

"My bag is hungry," said Ole Goat. Give me that stuff or I'll pitch you down the mountain with my bony, bony head."

"But your bag is full," protested Fox.

"There's always room for more," Ole Goat cried as he pawed the ground and lowered his head.

Fox sighed and, ducking, turned and bolted off down the trail. Ole Goat pushed the cart with its rag rugs and quilts into his hungry black bag.

And the bag grew bigger.

Ole Goat of Grede Mountain trotted on until he came to Porcupine pushing a wheelbarrow piled high with baskets of flowers.

"My bag is hungry," said Ole Goat. "Give me those flowers or I'll pitch you down the mountain with my bony, bony head."

"If you try to take them, you'll be sorry," said Porcupine, stamping her feet and bristling.

Ole Goat pawed the ground and lowered his head.

"All right. All right. If you can fit them into your bag, take them!" said Porcupine

Porcupine's eyes popped wide in amazement as Ole Goat squeezed the wheelbarrow and all the flowers into his hungry black bag.

And the bag grew bigger and bigger.

Ole Goat of Grede Mountain trotted on down the path until he came to Rabbit, who was so heaped over with pots and pans that he could scarcely see where he was going.

"My bag is hungry," said Ole Goat. "Give me that stuff or I'll pitch you down the mountain with my bony, bony head."

"There are too many pots and pans even for a goat!" Rabbit said as he dumped his load on the ground.

"I'll never have enough," said Ole Goat.

He crammed the pots and pans into his hungry black bag.

And it grew bigger and bigger and bigger.

Ole Goat of Grede Mountain trotted on down the trail until he came to Raccoon carrying a rake, a hoe, and a shovel under one arm and a broom and a mop under the other.

"My bag is hungry," bellowed Old Goat. "Give me those things or I'll pitch you down the mountain with my bony, bony head."

"But I must sell them to buy food for my children," said Raccoon.

"Your children mean nothing to me," said Ole Goat as he lowered his head and pawed the ground.

Raccoon dropped everything and scrambled up a nearby tree.

Ole Goat stuck the rake, the hoe, the shovel, the broom, and the mop into his hungry black bag.

And the bag grew bigger and bigger and bigger and bigger.

It was then that Bear came lumbering along, wearing a cocked hat with a long feather.

"My bag is hungry," bellowed Ole Goat.

"I am sorry," drawled Bear, "but I have nothing to feed it."

"Then give me your hat or I'll pitch you down the mountain with a butt of my bony, bony head."

"Oh, dear," drawled Bear. "When will you learn that you have more than enough?"

Ole Goat charged toward Bear. Bear threw his hat into the air. Ole Goat grabbed for the hat, bumped into his black bag, and lost his balance.

Down the mountainside he rolled. Over and over he rolled. The black bag tumbled after him, scattering the table, the cart, the quilts, the rag rugs, the pots, the pans, the flowers, the rake, the hoe, the shovel, the broom, and the mop. Ole Goat landed in mud up to his beard.

It didn't take long before Owl, Fox, Porcupine, Rabbit, and Raccoon had reclaimed their things. Thanking Bear, they went on their way to the market.

"Greedy goats should get what they deserve," said Bear as he draped the empty black bag on Ole Goat's head.